Here's what kids have to say to
Mary Pope Osborne, author of
the Magic Tree House series:

WOW! You have an imagination like no other.
—Adam W.

*I love your books. If you stop writing books, it will
be like losing a best friend.*—Ben M.

*I think you are the real Morgan le Fay. There is
always magic in your books.*—Erica Y.

*One day I was really bored and I didn't want to
read. . . . I looked in your book. I read a sentence,
and it was interesting. So I read some more, until
the book was done. It was so good I read more and
more. Then I had read all of your books, and now
I hope you write lots more.*—Danai K.

*I always read [your books] over and over . . .
1 time, 2 times, 3 times, 4 times. . . .*—Yuan C.

*You are my best author in the world. I love your
books. I read all the time. I read everywhere. My
mom is like freaking out.*—Ellen C.

*I hope you make
mine's life.*—Riki

Teachers and librarians love
Magic Tree House® books, too!

Thank you for opening faraway places and times to my class through your books. They have given me the chance to bring in additional books, materials, and videos to share with the class.
—J. Cameron

It excites me to see how involved [my fourth-grade reading class] is in your books. . . . I would do anything to get my students more involved, and this has done it.—C. Rutz

I discovered your books last year. . . . WOW! Our students have gone crazy over them. I can't order enough copies! . . . Thanks for contributing so much to children's literature!—C. Kendziora

I first came across your Magic Tree House series when my son brought one home. . . . I have since introduced this great series to my class. They have absolutely fallen in love with these books! . . . My students are now asking me for more independent reading time to read them. Your stories have inspired even my most struggling readers.—M. Payne

I love how I can go beyond the [Magic Tree House] books and use them as springboards for other learning.—R. Gale

We have enjoyed your books all year long. We check your Web site to find new information. We pull our map down to find the areas where the adventures take place. My class always chimes in at key parts of the story. It feels good to hear my students ask for a book and cheer when a new book comes out.—J. Korinek

Our students have "Magic Tree House fever." I can't keep your books on the library shelf. —J. Rafferty

Your books truly invite children into the pleasure of reading. Thanks for such terrific work.—S. Smith

The children in the fourth grade even hide the [Magic Tree House] books in the library so that they will be able to find them when they are ready to check them out.—K. Mortensen

My Magic Tree House books are never on the bookshelf because they are always being read by my students. Thank you for creating such a wonderful series.—K. Mahoney

Dear Readers,

*After I finished Magic Tree House® #22,
<u>Revolutionary War on Wednesday</u>, I decided
I wanted to write about pioneer times on the
prairie frontier. As I always do, I went to the
library for research. I read many nonfiction
books about prairie pioneers. One day,
I found a collection of true stories about
women who had lived on the Kansas frontier
in the late 1800s. When I read a passage
about a tornado roaring toward a prairie
schoolhouse, I got very excited. I'd always
wanted to write about a tornado—and I'd
been thinking about setting my new book in
a prairie schoolhouse! Now I could combine
these two ideas—and be true to real life.*

*I hope you'll enjoy your journey with Jack
and Annie to the Kansas frontier. But when
the wind starts to blow—watch out!*

All my best,

Mary Pope Osborne

Twister on Tuesday

by Mary Pope Osborne

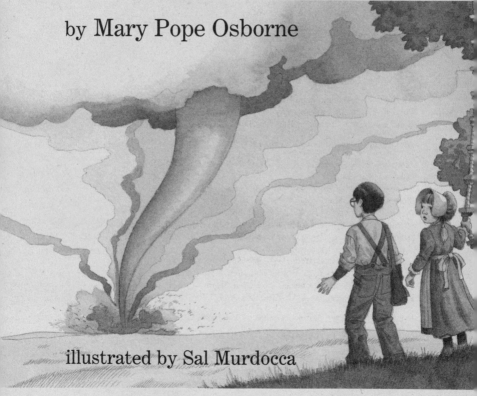

illustrated by Sal Murdocca

A STEPPING STONE BOOK™

Random House 🏠 New York

www.randomhouse.com/magictreehouse

Library of Congress Cataloging-in-Publication Data
Osborne, Mary Pope.
Twister on Tuesday / by Mary Pope Osborne ;
illustrated by Sal Murdocca.
p.   cm. — (Magic tree house ; #23) "A Stepping stone book."
SUMMARY: When Jack and Annie travel back to the Kansas prairie in search of
"something to learn," they gain an understanding of how hard life was for pioneers
and they experience the terror of a tornado.
ISBN 978-0-679-89069-0 (trade) — ISBN 978-0-679-99069-7 (lib. bdg.)
[1. Time travel—Fiction. 2. Frontier and pioneer life—Kansas—Fiction.
3. Tornadoes—Fiction. 4. Kansas—Fiction. 5. Magic—Fiction. 6. Tree houses—
Fiction.] I. Murdocca, Sal, ill. II. Title. PZ7.O81167 Tw 2001 [Fic]—dc21 00-044535

Printed in the United States of America   March 2001   25 24 23 22

Random House, Inc.   New York, Toronto, London, Sydney, Auckland

For Peter Boyce,
who likes to read about twisters

Contents

Prologue

One summer day in Frog Creek, Pennsylvania, a mysterious tree house appeared in the woods.

Eight-year-old Jack and his seven-year-old sister, Annie, climbed into the tree house. They found that it was filled with books.

Jack and Annie soon discovered that the tree house was magic. It could take them to the places in the books. All they had to do was point to a picture and wish to go there.

Along the way, Jack and Annie discovered

that the tree house belongs to Morgan le Fay. Morgan is a magical librarian from Camelot, the long-ago kingdom of King Arthur. She travels through time and space, gathering books.

In Magic Tree House Books #5–8, Jack and Annie helped free Morgan from a spell. In Books #9–12, they solved four ancient riddles and became Master Librarians.

In Magic Tree House Books #13–16, Jack and Annie had to save four ancient stories from being lost forever.

In Magic Tree House Books #17–20, Jack and Annie freed a mysterious little dog from a magic spell.

In Magic Tree House Books #21–24, Jack and Annie have a new challenge. They must find four special kinds of writing for Morgan's library to help save Camelot. They are about to set off to find the third of these. . . .

1

Tuesday!

Jack opened his eyes. Sunlight streamed through his window.

"Tuesday!" he whispered. Morgan's note had told him and Annie to come back to the magic tree house on Tuesday. He could hardly wait to find out where she was sending them today!

Jack scrambled out of bed. He threw on his clothes. He packed his notebook and pencil into his backpack. Then he headed into the hall.

Jack bumped into Annie. She was dressed in jeans and a T-shirt.

"Tuesday!" they both whispered.

Together, they hurried down the stairs.

"Mom, Dad, we're going out for a few minutes!" Jack shouted.

"Don't you want breakfast first?" his dad called from the kitchen.

"When we get back!" said Annie.

They rushed out the front door. They ran down their street in the bright summer sunlight.

A warm wind gently shook the trees as Jack and Annie headed into the Frog Creek woods. Soon they came to the tallest tree in the woods. The magic tree house waited for them in the high branches. Jack and Annie grabbed the rope ladder and climbed up.

Inside the shady tree house, the note from Morgan was still on the floor:

Dear Jack and Annie,

Camelot is in trouble. To save the kingdom, please find these four special kinds of writing for my library:

Something to follow
Something to send
Something to learn
Something to lend

Thank you,
Morgan

"Okay," said Jack. "We have the first writing: *something to follow.*" He picked up a list from the Civil War.

"And we have the second," said Annie, "*something to send.*" She picked up a letter from the Revolutionary War.

"Now we need the third," said Jack, *"something to learn."*

"No problem," said Annie. She grabbed a book lying in the corner. "I hope we're not going to another war."

Jack and Annie looked at the cover. It showed a field of tall green grass.

The title was *Life on the Prairie.*

"The prairie?" said Annie. "We already went to the prairie the time we met Black Hawk."

"Yeah," said Jack, remembering their adventure with the Native American boy.

He opened the book and turned to a picture of an old-fashioned train crossing the prairie.

"Oh," he said. "I get it. Trains crossed the prairie *after* the pioneers came. When we went to the prairie before, Native Americans were the *only* people who lived there."

"So we must be going to pioneer time," said Annie.

"I think so," said Jack.

He pointed at the picture that showed the train crossing the prairie.

"I wish we could go there," he said.

The breeze picked up.

The wind started to blow.

The tree house started to spin.

It spun faster and faster.

Then everything was still.

Absolutely still.

2

Signs of Life

Jack opened his eyes.

He was wearing pants with suspenders and a shirt with the sleeves rolled up. In place of his backpack was a leather bag.

Annie was wearing a long dress and a sunbonnet.

"I like my hat," she said. "It'll keep the sun off my face."

"Yeah, except the sun's not shining," said Jack.

He and Annie looked out the window.

The sky was cloudy.

The tree house had landed in a small grove of trees near a creek. Beyond the trees was a wide, open prairie. Green grass and wild-flowers swayed in a chilly wind.

In the distance, a train puffed across the prairie. Sparks of fire came out of its smoke-stack. Huge clouds of black smoke billowed into the gray sky.

"Wow," said Jack.

He looked at the picture of the train in their book and read:

> **After the Civil War, the U.S. government built railroads to link the eastern and western parts of the country. By the 1870s, steam engines carried people across the Kansas prairie.**

Jack pulled out his notebook and wrote:

1870s—trains across Kansas

"Let's get going," said Annie. "We have to find that special writing for Morgan."

She started down the ladder.

Jack packed his things in his leather bag and climbed down after her.

When he stepped onto the ground, Jack looked toward the west.

The train was gone. Only a thin trail of smoke floated across the sky.

"That train was cool," said Jack.

"Yeah, and so is *that*," said Annie. She pointed in the other direction.

Far away, in the distance, a line of covered wagons rolled through the rippling grass. Their white coverings billowed in the breeze.

Jack pulled out the research book. He

found a picture of the wagon train. He read aloud:

> **Wagons were the most common way for families to travel west. They could carry clothes, tools, food, and water. A line of wagons was called a "wagon train." The white cloth coverings over**

the wagons also made them look
like sailing ships, or schooners. For
this reason, covered wagons were
sometimes called "prairie schooners."

Jack looked at the wagons again. They *did*
look like ships sailing across a rippling green
sea.

He wrote in his notebook:

covered wagons = prairie schooners

"Let's get a closer look," said Annie.

She took off across the grass.

Jack put away his things and ran after her. As they ran, the wind began to blow harder. The clouds overhead grew darker.

"Wait—wait!" Jack finally called to Annie. "We'll never catch up to it!"

They both stopped running. Panting, they watched the wagon train vanish over the horizon.

Jack took a deep breath.

"What now?" he said.

They looked around.

All Jack could see was the distant grove of trees with the tree house.

With the train and wagon train gone, there were no signs of life anywhere—no pioneer cabins, no Native American tepees.

"How can we find the special writing?" said Jack. "There's nothing out here."

"Oh yeah?" said Annie. "What's *that*?"

She pointed to a rusty pipe sticking out from the top of a small hill.

Streaming from the pipe was a column of black smoke.

"Oh, man," said Jack, "that's *definitely* a sign of life."

3

One-Room Schoolhouse

"Let's check it out," said Annie.

She and Jack walked up the little hill. At the top, they saw that the rusty pipe was rising out of a wooden roof.

They walked around to the other side of the hill.

Beneath the wooden roof was a door. The door seemed to open into the hill itself.

"What is this?" said Annie.

"Let's find out," said Jack.

He studied their research book until he
found a black-and-white photograph. The
photograph showed the same hill with the
door.

Jack read aloud:

> Since the prairie did not have many
> trees, wood was hard to find. So
> pioneers often made their houses out
> of sod bricks, which were blocks of
> earth cut out of the prairie. Sometimes
> a sod house was dug out of the side of
> a hill. It was called a "dugout."

Jack pulled out his notebook. He wrote:

sod bricks = blocks of earth

dugout = sod house carved out of hillside

Then Jack read more to Annie:

> Tornados, or twisters, are common on
> the prairie, so many dugouts had
> storm cellars. A storm cellar was like
> a rough basement below the ground.

18

**During a twister, a storm cellar is the
safest place to be.**

"Wow, maybe we'll see a twister," said
Annie.

"I hope not," said Jack. Then he read on:

**A pioneer family built *this* dugout
for a home. When they moved, the
dugout became a schoolhouse. The
schoolhouse had only one room. It
also had a storm cellar beneath it.**

Jack quickly wrote:

some dugouts have storm cellars

"Hey! This is the place!" said Annie.
Jack looked up from his writing.
"What place?" he asked.
"Where's the best place to find our special

19

writing—*something to learn?*" asked Annie.

Jack smiled.

"A school," he said.

Annie ran to the wooden door and knocked loudly.

A moment later, the door creaked open. A girl peeked out. Her hair was in a tight bun, as if she were a grownup. But she didn't look more than sixteen or seventeen years old.

"Hi, I'm Annie," said Annie. "This is my brother, Jack."

The girl opened the door wider.

"Hello, Jack and Annie," she said. "I'm your teacher, Miss Neely."

"*You're* the teacher?" said Jack. Miss Neely seemed way too young to be a teacher.

"Yes!" she said, smiling. "Come in. You're late."

4

Reading Lesson

It was warm and dry inside the schoolhouse. Several oil lamps lit the darkness.

"Class, meet Annie and Jack," the young teacher said.

What class? thought Jack.

There were only three kids.

On one bench sat a small boy and a girl. The boy looked about Annie's age. The girl looked a little younger. On another bench sat a tall boy. He was tough-looking.

"Welcome to our first day of school," said the young teacher.

"Today's your very first day?" said Annie.

"Yes, and our first day in this dugout. The family who lived here left for California a week ago," said Miss Neely.

Jack and Annie peered around the room.

The walls were made of dirt. The floor was made of wood. It was covered by a worn rug.

Miss Neely's desk was made from a barrel. A small coal stove was near her desk. A crate held a water jug, chalk, and two small blackboards.

"It's a nice school," Annie said politely.

"Thank you. We're very grateful for it," said Miss Neely. "And where do you live?"

"Well, we actually . . . ," Jack started. Then he stopped—he wasn't sure what to say.

"Actually, we don't live around here," Annie said. "We're passing through."

"You must be from the wagon train I saw this morning," Miss Neely said.

Annie nodded.

Jack smiled.

Good work, Annie, he thought.

"We can only stay a little while," he said.

"How exciting for you," said Miss Neely. "Heading west on a wagon train. Where are you going?"

"California," Annie said.

"California! That's wonderful! Isn't it, class?" Miss Neely said to the others.

"Yes, ma'am!" said the two younger children. The older boy barely nodded.

"Have you ever been to school before?" Miss Neely asked Annie.

"Yes, ma'am," Annie said. "We both know how to read and write. Jack's one of the best readers you'll ever meet."

"My! Isn't that wonderful, class?" said Miss Neely.

"Yes, ma'am!" said the younger children.

The older boy gave Jack a scowl.

"Not exactly the *best*," Jack said modestly.

"I love to read," said Miss Neely. "I'll read any book I can get my hands on."

"Me too," said Jack.

"Then perhaps you'd like to start off our first reading lesson of the school year," said Miss Neely.

"Sure," said Jack.

"Sit with Jeb, then," said Miss Neely, "and Annie, you sit with Kate and her brother, Will."

Will and Kate quickly made room for Annie on their bench.

But Jeb didn't move over for Jack, not even an inch.

Jack barely had room to sit. He took a deep breath and sat on the end of the bench.

Miss Neely handed Jack a book.

"This is our only reader," she said. "It's called the McGuffey Reader. Please read the first two lines of the poem on page fifty."

"Oh, um . . . sure, ma'am," said Jack.

He turned to page fifty. He pushed his glasses into place. Then he read aloud:

"Twinkle, twinkle, little star.
How I wonder what you are."

"Very good!" said Miss Neely. "Now pass the reader to Jeb."

Jack handed the book to Jeb.

"Jeb, please read the next two lines," said Miss Neely.

The older boy cleared his throat and stared at the page.

"Maybe Jeb can't read," Will said in a kind voice to Miss Neely.

Jeb's face got red.

"Shut up, Will," he muttered.

"Oh!" said Miss Neely. She looked confused.

Jack felt sorry for Jeb. He wanted to give him some help.

Barely moving his lips, Jack whispered, *"Up above the world so high, like a diamond—"*

Jeb turned on Jack with an angry look.

"I don't need your help," he said.

"Now, Jeb, don't get mad," said Miss Neely. "And, Jack, you shouldn't give people the answers."

"I'm sorry," said Jack.

Miss Neely sighed and pulled out her pocket watch. She was starting to look tired.

"Why don't you all go outside and have

your noon meal?" she said. "I'll stay in and prepare for our next lesson."

Miss Neely opened the door of the sod hut.

Annie, Kate, and Will bounced up from their seats and started cheerfully out of the schoolroom.

Jack turned to Jeb.

"Hey, sorry for what happened," Jack said.

Jeb just glared at him and didn't say anything.

"Come on, Jack!" Annie called outside the hut. "Kate wants us to eat with them!"

Jack hurried out the door. He didn't look back at Jeb.

5

Bully

The air outside was strangely still. The dark clouds still hovered in the distance.

"Storm's coming," said Will.

"We have to eat quickly, before it starts to rain," said Kate. She and Will sat down on the grass.

Annie and Jack sat beside them.

Will opened a small burlap sack. He took out four lumpy objects. They looked like dark rocks.

"Hey, there's one here for each of us!" said Kate.

"One *what*?" asked Annie, frowning.

"Sweet potatoes!" said Will. He gave a potato each to Kate, Annie, and Jack.

"Um—no thanks," said Jack, trying to give his back. "We don't want to take your lunch."

"We have enough! Keep it!" said Kate.

"What do you do with it?" asked Annie, holding up her potato.

Kate laughed.

"Just bite!" she said. "Like this—"

Kate and Will bit into their cold sweet potatoes as if they were apples.

"Cool," said Annie. She took a big bite out of her potato, too.

But Jack just held on to his. He didn't

quite feel like eating the cold, brown potato.

Out of the corner of his eye, he saw Jeb sitting by himself. The big kid didn't seem to have any lunch at all.

Jack thought he'd try to be friends one more time.

"Hey, Jeb," he called out. "I'm not hungry. You want my sweet potato?"

Jeb gave Jack a mean look.

"I could have brought my own lunch if I wanted to eat," he said.

"Oh, sure," said Jack.

Jeb narrowed his eyes.

"You making fun again?" he said. "I'm warning you. Do that one more time, and I'll fight you."

Jack couldn't believe it. This kid took everything he said the wrong way!

"Hey!" Annie said. "Leave my brother alone. You're nothing but a bully, Jeb."

"Annie, stay out of this," said Jack.

But Jeb just laughed. Then he stood up and walked back into the schoolhouse.

Jack felt angry. He hoped they would find the special writing soon so they could leave.

Will seemed to have read Jack's mind.

"Don't worry about him," Will said to Jack. "He's never been to school before."

"Oh, so he's embarrassed," said Annie.

"Why hasn't he been to school?" said Jack.

"Because he has to work in the fields all the time," said Will.

"I heard him tell Miss Neely he walked five miles to get here today," Kate said. "So he must have really wanted to come."

"Wow," said Annie. "How far did you and Will walk?"

"Only two," said Kate.

"Two what?" asked Annie.

"Miles," said Kate.

"Two miles," Jack repeated.

The prairie kids nodded.

"It must be lonely living out here," Annie said.

Will and Kate nodded again.

"Do you live in a sod house?" Jack asked.

"We used to," said Will. "But it was always dirty. So our pa built us a log cabin."

"He cut trees near the creek," said Kate. "Then he made the cabin by hand."

Before Annie or Jack could ask another question, thunder cracked in the sky. Then rain started to fall. It fell fast and hard.

Everyone jumped up.

"Come in! Come in!" Miss Neely called from the doorway.

They ran back inside. The wind slammed the door behind them with a BANG.

6

Grasshopper Attack?

Inside the lamplit hut, it was dry and cozy.

Jack sat back on his bench. He didn't dare look at Jeb.

"It's time for our writing lesson now," Miss Neely said. "I'm going to give you each a slate and a pen."

She handed out the slates. They looked like small blackboards set in wooden frames.

Next she gave everyone a slate pen. Each pen was a thin piece of chalk.

Miss Neely opened the McGuffey Reader.

"While you were eating your noon meal, I copied a poem from the book," she said. "Now I want *you* to copy it."

Miss Neely held her own slate board up for them all to see:

> 'Tis a lesson you should heed,
>
> Try, try again;
>
> If at first you don't succeed,
>
> Try, try again.

Jack quickly started copying the words. Out of the corner of his eye, he saw Jeb writing very slowly. It took the older boy a long time just to write the letter T.

Jack slowed down, too. He didn't want Jeb to think he was showing off.

Suddenly, loud thumping sounds came

from overhead. It sounded as if someone were throwing stones against the roof.

"Oh no! Grasshopper attack!" screamed Kate. She covered her head.

"Grasshopper attack!" cried Will. He covered his head, too.

"Be calm, everyone!" said Miss Neely.

What's a grasshopper attack? What are they talking about? Jack wondered.

Even Jeb seemed worried. As Miss Neely started toward the door, he said, "Don't open it! They'll come in!"

Has everyone gone crazy? Jack thought. *How can grasshoppers hurt anyone?*

Miss Neely opened the door and looked out. A moment later, she stuck her head back in and closed the door.

"It's all right," she said. "It's only hailstones."

"What's that?" said Annie.

"Hailstones are small pieces of frozen rain. Sometimes they fall to earth during a thunderstorm," said Miss Neely.

"Why did Will and Kate yell, 'Grasshopper attack!'?" Jack asked.

"Because last spring, grasshoppers *did* attack us," said Miss Neely.

"Yes! Millions and millions of them came out of the sky," said Will. "It looked like a huge, shiny cloud."

"They covered every inch of ground!" said Kate. "They ate everything!"

"They ate all our crops," said Will, "our turnips and fruit trees and watermelons."

"They even ate our clothes and bed-sheets!" said Kate.

"Yuck," said Annie.

"Oh, man," said Jack. He'd never heard of

a grasshopper attack before.

"It was very scary," said Kate.

"But remember how we replanted and everyone helped everyone else?" said Miss Neely.

Kate and Will nodded.

"We must try to hold on to the good memories," Miss Neely said gently, "and let go of the bad ones."

"Yes, ma'am," said Kate.

Everyone was quiet for a moment. Then the sound of the hailstones died away.

"Let's go back to our lesson now," said Miss Neely.

They all returned to their writing.

Even working as slowly as he could, Jack finished first. He showed his copy of the poem to Miss Neely.

"Good work, Jack," she said. "We can all learn from these words, can't we?"

"Yes, ma'am," said Jack.

"Hey, this is it, Jack!" Annie blurted out. *"Something to learn!"*

Miss Neely looked puzzled.

But Jack smiled. He knew what Annie was talking about: *They had their special writing. They could go home!*

Jack stood up.

"Excuse me, ma'am, but I'm afraid we have to leave," he said.

"So soon?" said Miss Neely.

"Yes, we have to go back to our parents," said Annie.

"May I take my slate with us?" Jack asked.

"Please do," said Miss Neely. "Use it on

your trip to California to practice your writing."

"Thanks!" said Jack with a big smile. He put the slate in his leather bag. "We learned a lot, ma'am."

"I'm glad you had a chance to come to school," said Miss Neely. "Good-bye and good luck."

"Good luck to you, too," said Annie.

"Bye!" Will and Kate called out.

"Bye!" said Jack and Annie.

As they went out the door, Jack glanced at Jeb. He felt sorry for the older boy. He tried one last time to be friends.

"Bye, Jeb," he said.

But the boy wouldn't even look at him.

Jack gently closed the door to the schoolhouse.

He breathed a sigh of relief. He was glad to get away from Jeb's anger.

"That's weird," said Annie. "Look at the sky."

As Jack turned away from the schoolhouse door, he caught his breath.

The sky *did* look weird—really weird.

7

Twister!

The black clouds had taken on an odd greenish color. They all seemed to be going in different directions.

"Do you think it's a grasshopper attack?" Annie asked nervously.

"No, I think it's some more weird weather, like that hailstorm," said Jack. "Let's go before it gets worse."

As they started back to the tree house, the wind picked up.

Jack and Annie looked over their shoulders. The greenish clouds had dipped down close to the prairie.

"I feel like something awful is about to happen," said Annie.

"Hurry!" said Jack. "Run!"

He and Annie started running through the grass. When they got to the ladder of the tree house, they looked back.

In the distance, twisting black clouds had dropped out of the storm clouds. They were swirling into a funnel shape.

The dark funnel started twisting across the prairie.

Jack's heart nearly jumped out of his chest.

"It's a twister!" he said.

"Oh no!" cried Annie.

The twister was whirling and tearing across the grass.

"Let's get out of here!" said Jack. He grabbed the rope ladder and started up.

"Wait!" said Annie. "We have to help Miss Neely and the other kids!"

"They have a storm cellar!" Jack said. "That's what our book said!"

"Yeah, but it's only their first day in the dugout! They might not know about it!" said Annie. "There was a rug on the floor!"

Annie is right, Jack thought.

He looked up at the tree house. All they had to do was climb up and leave, and *they'd* be safe.

But what about Miss Neely? What about Will and Kate and Jeb?

"Okay!" said Jack. He jumped down from the ladder. "Let's go back!"

He and Annie started running back toward the schoolhouse.

They ran as fast as they could across the prairie.

The roaring sound of the twister followed them.

Suddenly, the wind threw them to the ground!

Jack clutched the tall grass, trying to stand. When he got up, he grabbed Annie's hand. He pulled her up, too.

With all his might, Jack held on to Annie and pulled her along.

The roaring twister came closer and closer.

The wind ripped up grass and earth around them. The roar grew deafening.

Jack and Annie could barely stay on their feet. Finally, they reached the dugout.

They tried to open the door, but it wouldn't budge.

They banged on the door with their fists.

"Let us in!" Annie shouted.

No one opened the door.

"They can't hear us!" yelled Jack.

But the sound of the twister drowned out his voice.

8

Get Below!

Suddenly, the schoolhouse door blew off its hinges! It went flying through the air!

Jack grabbed Annie and pulled her into the dugout.

Inside, the benches were overturned. The room was a mess.

Miss Neely and the three kids were pressed against the dirt wall. Kate and Will screamed as the winds whipped around the room.

Miss Neely hugged Kate. Jeb held on to Will.

"Get in the cellar!" Jack yelled.

"What cellar?" shouted Miss Neely.

Together, Jack and Annie pulled the rug off the floor and uncovered the cellar door.

They grabbed the door and tried to open it, but the wind was blowing too hard.

Suddenly, Jeb was beside them. He pulled the door open. A ladder led down into the cellar.

One by one, Will, Kate, Miss Neely, and Annie went down the ladder.

Jack waited for Jeb to go down.

"Go! Go!" Jeb shouted.

Jack climbed down into the cellar.

Jeb came last. He closed the door behind him, leaving everyone in total darkness.

The twister roared fiercely above them. It sounded like a train barreling right through the schoolhouse!

As the twister roared and howled, Jack couldn't think. He couldn't feel. He was totally swept up in the howl of the wind.

Then, just as Jack felt he would disappear in the roar of the twister, the noise died down.

And then it was silent.

No one spoke for a moment in the blackness. Then Annie broke the silence.

"Are we still alive?" she whispered.

Everyone laughed.

"Yes, I think we are," said Miss Neely.

9

All Clear

Jeb pushed open the cellar door. Daylight streamed in. He looked out.

"All clear," he said.

Jeb crawled out of the cellar. Jack followed him, then Annie, Will, Kate, and Miss Neely.

The sky was gray above them. The twister had torn the roof off the dugout and sucked everything out, even the rug.

They all stared in shock at the empty space.

Then Miss Neely smiled.

"Well, at least we are all safe," she said.

They stepped out of the hut. The air was thick with dust and bits of grass.

The twister had cut a wide path of dirt and destruction across the prairie. It was still whirling away on the horizon.

Everyone watched silently as the twister became long and thin, like a piece of rope. Then it vanished completely.

Miss Neely turned to Jack and Annie.

"You saved our lives," she said.

"Thank you!" said Will.

"Thank you!" said Kate, hugging Annie.

"Jeb actually opened the cellar door," said Jack.

"Yes! Thank you, too, Jeb!" said Miss Neely.

The older boy only scowled.

"I hope you can get a new school," said Annie.

"We will," said Miss Neely. "Just as we planted our fields again after the grasshopper attack, we'll build our school again after the twister. If at first you don't succeed, try, try again."

Jack thought Miss Neely was one of the bravest people he'd ever met.

"You're a good teacher," he said shyly.

"I love teaching," she said. "It's a job that lasts forever. Whatever you teach children today travels with them far into the future."

"That's true!" said Annie.

Jack smiled.

"Well, we better leave—again," he said.

"Bye!" Everyone waved, except Jeb.

Jack and Annie started across the prairie, back toward the tree house.

They hadn't gone far when Jack heard someone shout his name. He turned around.

It was Jeb.

"Wait!" the older boy yelled. He had a fierce look on his face. He started running toward them.

"Oh no," Jack breathed. Did Jeb still want to fight?

"Leave us alone!" Annie said angrily.

"Shh, Annie," said Jack. "Let's see what he wants."

When Jeb got close to them, he stopped. He looked right at Jack.

"Why did you come back?" he asked.

"We wanted to tell you about the storm cellar," said Jack.

"How did you know about that cellar?" Jeb said.

Jack pulled their research book out of his leather bag.

"We read about it in this book," he said.

Jeb stared at the book. Then he sighed.

"I aim to read someday, too," he said. "That looks like a good book."

Jack didn't know what to say. He was still afraid of making Jeb mad. So he just nodded.

"My ma and pa were too poor to go to school," said Jeb. "They want me to go. But I'm getting started mighty late."

"It's not too late," said Jack.

"It's *never* too late," said Annie.

Jeb narrowed his eyes.

"If you ever come back through here . . . ," he said.

"Yes . . . ?" Jack asked carefully. Was Jeb about to threaten him again?

"Maybe I'll be able to read that book of yours," Jeb said.

Jack sighed and smiled.

"I know you will," he said.

Jeb smiled back. He had a nice smile.

"Thanks for coming back to rescue us," he said to both Jack and Annie. "Too bad you can't stay. I reckon we'd all be good friends if you did."

"I reckon we would," said Annie.

Jeb nodded. Then he turned and ran back to join the others.

Suddenly, the sun broke through the clouds. The wildflowers danced in a gentle breeze.

"Ready?" said Annie.

Jack just stood there, staring at the sunlit prairie.

"*Jack?* Ready to go?" Annie asked.

In that moment, Jack actually hated to leave. But he nodded slowly and said, "Let's go."

He and Annie took off through the bright, sparkling grass. They ran to the small grove of trees near the creek.

They climbed up the rope ladder and scrambled into the tree house.

Annie picked up their Pennsylvania book.

"I wish we could go there," she said.

This time the wind did *not* start to blow.

The tree house simply started to spin on its own.

It spun faster and faster.

Then everything was still.

Absolutely still.

10

The Third Writing

Jack opened his eyes.

Morning light filled the tree house.

He and Annie were wearing their own clothes again.

"Home," said Annie, smiling.

Jack looked out the window.

He saw their nice, cozy house in the distance, their lawn, their sidewalk, their paved street.

"Life here is pretty easy compared to pioneer life," said Jack.

"We're lucky," said Annie.

Jack reached into his bag and pulled out the small slate.

"Our third writing," he said. He added the poem to the list from the Civil War and the letter from the Revolutionary War.

"You did just what that poem says you should do," said Annie.

"What do you mean?" Jack asked.

"*If at first you don't succeed, try, try again,*" Annie said. "You kept trying to make friends with Jeb. In the end, you did."

"I guess you're right," said Jack.

"We have to get only one more special writing for Morgan's library," said Annie.

"I wonder how that will help save Camelot?" said Jack.

Annie shrugged.

"It's a mystery," she said.

She and Jack looked around the tree house.

"Look—" Annie picked up a piece of paper lying in the corner. She read aloud:

Come back early Wednesday morning.

"Wednesday? Man, that's *tomorrow*!" said Jack.

"So?" said Annie. She started down the rope ladder.

"Not much time to recover," said Jack, pulling on his backpack.

"Recover from what?" Annie said.

"The twister," said Jack.

"Oh yeah, I'd almost forgotten about that," said Annie.

Jack smiled.

Actually, the nightmare of the twister was fading from his memory, too.

We must try to hold on to the good memories, Miss Neely had said, *and let go of the bad ones.*

The kindness of Will and Kate, making friends with Jeb, the courage of Miss Neely— *these* memories, Jack thought, he would never forget.

MORE FACTS ABOUT TWISTERS

- Twisters, or tornados, are the fastest winds on earth.
- Twisters can travel at speeds up to 200 miles per hour.
- The spinning winds act like a giant vacuum cleaner as they move across the earth.
- Almost 1,000 tornados hit the United States each year.

MORE FACTS ABOUT
PIONEER LIFE ON THE PRAIRIE

From the mid-1800s through the 1880s, thousands of pioneers traveled by wagon across America. Most were headed for the territories of Oregon and California. But a number stopped and settled on the Kansas frontier. They made dugouts and broke up the hard ground to plant crops. These pioneers faced windstorms and dust storms, a shortage of water, and grasshopper plagues. In spite of the hardships, they set up small schools so their children could learn the three R's: "reading, 'riting, and 'rithmetic." Children of varied ages often learned together. It was not unusual for teachers to be as young as 15 or 16 years old.

MORE FACTS ABOUT
PIONEER SCHOOLBOOKS

The most popular American schoolbooks of the 1880s were called McGuffey Readers. They were put together by a schoolteacher from Ohio named William Holmes McGuffey. Poems such as "Mary Had a Little Lamb," "Twinkle, Twinkle, Little Star," and "If at First You Don't Succeed" became part of American life because they were in the McGuffey Readers.

Webster's Spelling Book was another significant reference in early American schools. It taught people who'd come here from all over the world how to spell words in the English language.

Have you read the Magic Tree House book
in which Jack and Annie are whisked
back to colonial times and meet
George Washington himself?

MAGIC TREE HOUSE® #22

REVOLUTIONARY WAR
ON WEDNESDAY

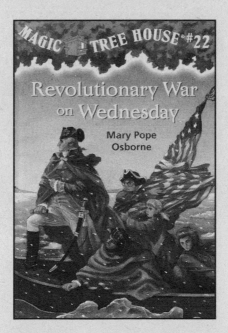

Don't miss the next Magic Tree House book,
in which Jack and Annie are shaken up
during their adventure in San Francisco . . .

MAGIC TREE HOUSE® #24

EARTHQUAKE IN THE EARLY MORNING

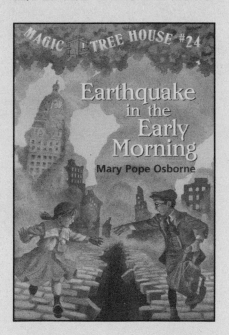

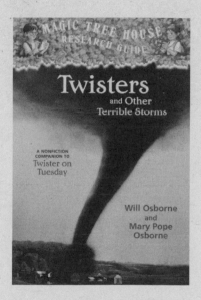

Discover the facts
behind the fiction with the

MAGIC TREE HOUSE®
RESEARCH GUIDES

The must-have, all-true companions for your favorite Magic Tree House® adventures!

Get your
Official
Magic Tree House
PASSPORT!
www.magictreehouse.com

AROUND THE WORLD
WITH JACK AND ANNIE

Around the World with Jack and Annie!

You have traveled to far away places and have been
on countless Magic Tree House adventures.
Now is your chance to receive an official
Magic Tree House passport and collect official stamps
for each destination from around the world!

Get your exclusive Magic Tree House Passport!*

Send your name, street address, city, state, zip code, and date of birth to:
The Magic Tree House Passport, Random House Children's Books,
Marketing Department, 1745 Broadway, 10th Floor, New York, NY 10019

OR log on to **www.magictreehouse.com/passport**
to download and print your passport now!

Collect Official Magic Tree House Stamps:

Log on to **www.magictreehouse.com** to submit your answer to the
trivia questions below. If you answer correctly, you will automatically
receive your official stamp for Book 23: *Twister on Tuesday.*

1. What are small pieces of frozen rain called?

2. What's the title of the only book in the prairie schoolhouse?

3. What term means "a line of covered wagons"?

*One passport per person. No purchase necessary. While supplies last. Allow 6 to 8 weeks for delivery.

Read all the Magic Tree House adventures for a chance to collect them all!
RHCB

Are you a fan of the Magic Tree House® series?

Visit our

MAGIC TREE HOUSE®

Web site

at

www.magictreehouse.com

Exciting sneak previews of the next book.
Games, puzzles, and other fun activities.
Contests with super prizes.
And much more!

Guess what?
Jack and Annie have a musical CD!

For more information about
MAGIC TREE HOUSE: THE MUSICAL
(including how to order the CD!),
visit www.mthmusical.com.